LUNA the LION

Written by
Laura Elizabeth Necci

Illustrated by
Sarah K. Turner

Halo
PUBLISHING
INTERNATIONAL

Love,
Kristina
McDonald

Copyright © 2023 Laura Elizabeth Necci, All rights reserved.
Illustrated by Sarah K. Turner

No part of this publication may be reproduced, stored in a retrieval system or transmitted in any form or by any means, electronic, mechanical, photocopying, recording or otherwise, without prior permission of Halo Publishing International.

For permission requests, write to the publisher, addressed "Attention: Permissions Coordinator," at the address below.

Halo Publishing International
8000 W Interstate 10, #600
San Antonio, Texas 78230

First Edition, January 2023
Printed in the United States of America
ISBN: 978-1-63765-299-2
Library of Congress Control Number: 2022915774

Halo Publishing International is a self-publishing company that publishes adult fiction and non-fiction, children's literature, self-help, spiritual, and faith-based books. Do you have a book idea you would like us to consider publishing? Please visit www.halopublishing.com for more information.

To my family, who taught me that being true to yourself and facing your fears are the only ways to roam through life.

To my mom, Fran; dad, Jim; and sisters Katie and Christina. The love we have for each other helps us conquer any challenge and obstacle that is thrown our way. Thank you for your unconditional love and being my pride in all adventures throughout this life.

To my cousin Michelle, who pushed me and taught me how to bring light and love to those who are different and unapologetically themselves. This book could have not happened without you. I know you are enjoying all heaven has to offer, and you are dancing among the stars. I will carry you in my heart always.

And lastly, to the loving parents, siblings, and teachers of individuals who are on the autism spectrum. The support and love you give every day does not go unnoticed or unappreciated. Keep believing, pushing, raising awareness, and accepting these beautiful individuals.

Out in the jungle, where the moon shines above, lived the most pristine pride who were all filled with love. The pack was quite noble, respected, and fair, but there was always one cub who seemed to quite not be there.

Luna the Lion always did what she was told, but although she tried hard, she could not fit the mold. Her brothers and sisters loved to chase the sunrise, and the loud sounds and textures never took them by surprise.

But our Luna the Lion could not handle the lights, and the loud sounds and textures simply gave her the frights. She wanted to feel what it was to belong, but she did not understand why she sang a much different song.

Then, one day, our Luna was out walking with her pride, along with her siblings and parents by her side. When suddenly a rain like no other ensued, and the mud on the ground turned as sticky as glue. Luna's family, unbothered, kept trekking along when Luna felt panicked, trapped, and all wrong.

Just when Luna was about to give up, her mother looked back and saw how, for Luna, this was tough. Her mother found Luna and proceeded to say, "I know this is hard, but keep moving ahead. The roads may be rocky, but do not lower your head. No matter what comes or whatever you face, each person's struggles and journeys will help them find their true place."

So, although it was tough and as sticky as glue, Luna had trouble, but she knew what to do. She lifted her head and got out of that place, and with her family's love and support there was not a thing she couldn't face. Our Luna, who struggled and sang to a different beat, felt proud of herself and her lack of defeat. She strolled on with her pack in the pride's land that day, where their journey continued into the land of Principe.

The tall grass was limber; the ocean was blue; there were many green trees, which for Luna was new. As Luna and her family approached this new land, it was apparent they were no longer in the pride's land. The starling birds were loudly chirping and fluttering overhead while they were tending to their young right above Luna's head. Luna looked around at her family, distraught and confused; where they were hearing music, she was not amused.

All Luna was hearing, while the birds' melody played, was pots and pans banging with aggression and rage. Luna was panicked and did not know how to face the mud and the challenge of the sounds in this place. And just when our Luna was starting to tear, her mother looked back, making sure Luna could hear. "I know this is hard, but keep moving ahead. The roads may be rocky, but do not lower your head. No matter what comes or whatever you face, each person's struggles and journeys will help them find their true place."

So, although it was loud, and the grass was green and tall. With her family by her side, Luna knew she could not fall. She lifted her head and got out of that place and remembered that, with love and support, there was not a thing she could not face. Our Luna, who struggled and sang to a different beat, was proud that with her family's love she overcame defeat. Although she has struggles that are not the norm, with her family by her side, she can face any storm.

Luna's family approached their home during a sunset that day, and her mother, who'd noticed, looked back, panicked and gray. The bright lights bothered Luna, just like mud, and they made her all fearful like the birds' sounds from above. But Luna's mother was surprised when she turned back around. Luna was looking at her mother, not making a sound. Our Luna was standing with a gleam in her eye, but not from tears, more a laugh and a sigh. Luna looked towards her mother with a big smile and replied, "Although it was tough and as sticky as glue, and as loud as the birds in the tree's morning dew, it is as bright as can be on an African sky, but I am grateful and happy. Let me tell you why."

"Yes, I had trouble, but I knew what to do. I lifted my head and got out of that place, and I know, with your love and support, there is not a thing I cannot face. Thank you for being there through the good and the bad, during my big challenges and small challenges, whether I´m happy or sad. Without your love and understanding, I wouldn´t know what to do. You love Luna for Luna, and I love you for you."

CPSIA information can be obtained
at www.ICGtesting.com
Printed in the USA
LVHW071737161222
735290LV00009B/576